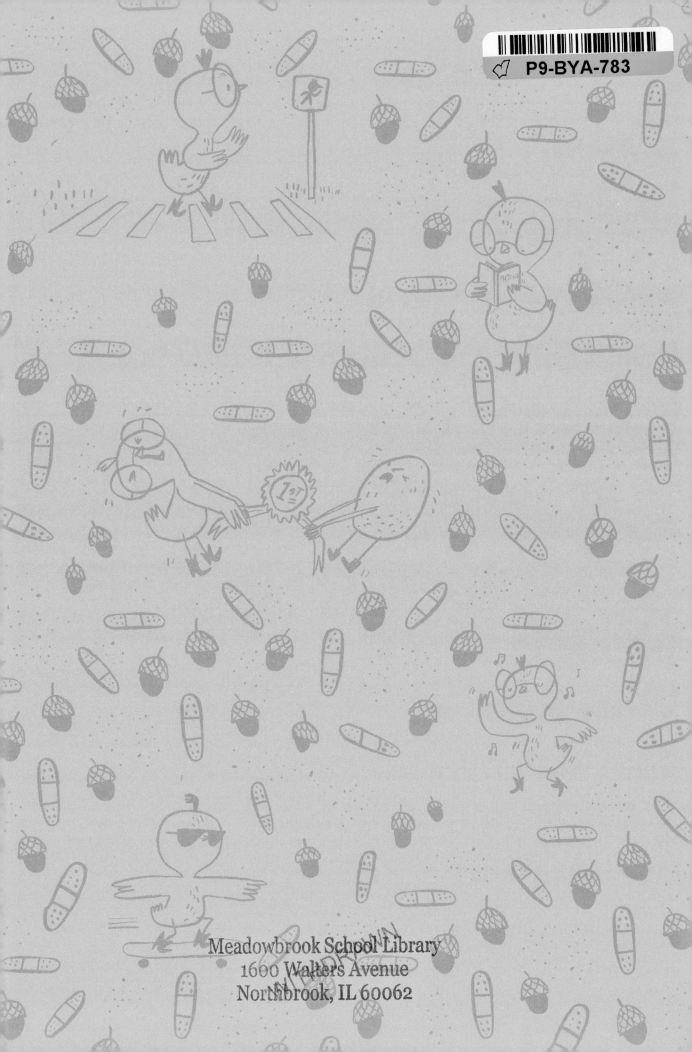

CHICKEN LITTLE

THE REAL AND TOTALLY TRUE TALE

WHO ARE YOU CALLING "LITTLE"?

SAM WEDELICH

SCHOLASTIC PRESS • NEW YORK

"LITTLE" implies Young and SMALL. I am NOT a BABY. BABIES aRE Easily SCARED and I'M NOT AFRAID of ANYTHING!

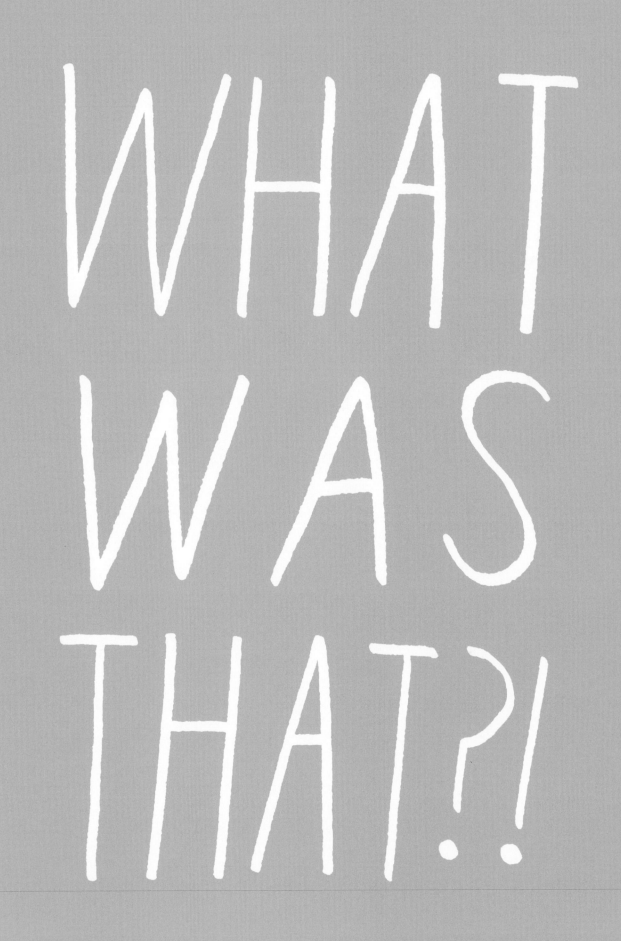

IS THE COAST CLEAR? NOTHING LOOKS DANGEROUS?

CHICKEN LITTLE LOOKED LOW.

ME? NO!
I AM A BLANKET
OF GAS HELD by
the PULL oF GRAVITY.
I DO NOT FALL.

WELL...
METEORS, STARS,
RAIN, SNOW, HAIL!!
USUALLY YOU TURN
WHITE OR GRAY FOR
THAT STUFF, BUT WHO
KNOWS WHAT YOU'RE
CAPABLE OF... MAYBE
YOU COULD START
FALLING AT ANY
TIME!

NO.
HONESTLY, I'M
FINE.

JUST CHECKING IN WITH THE SKY TO MAKE SURE IT'S NOT FALLING.
WHAT?! THE SKY IS FALLING?!

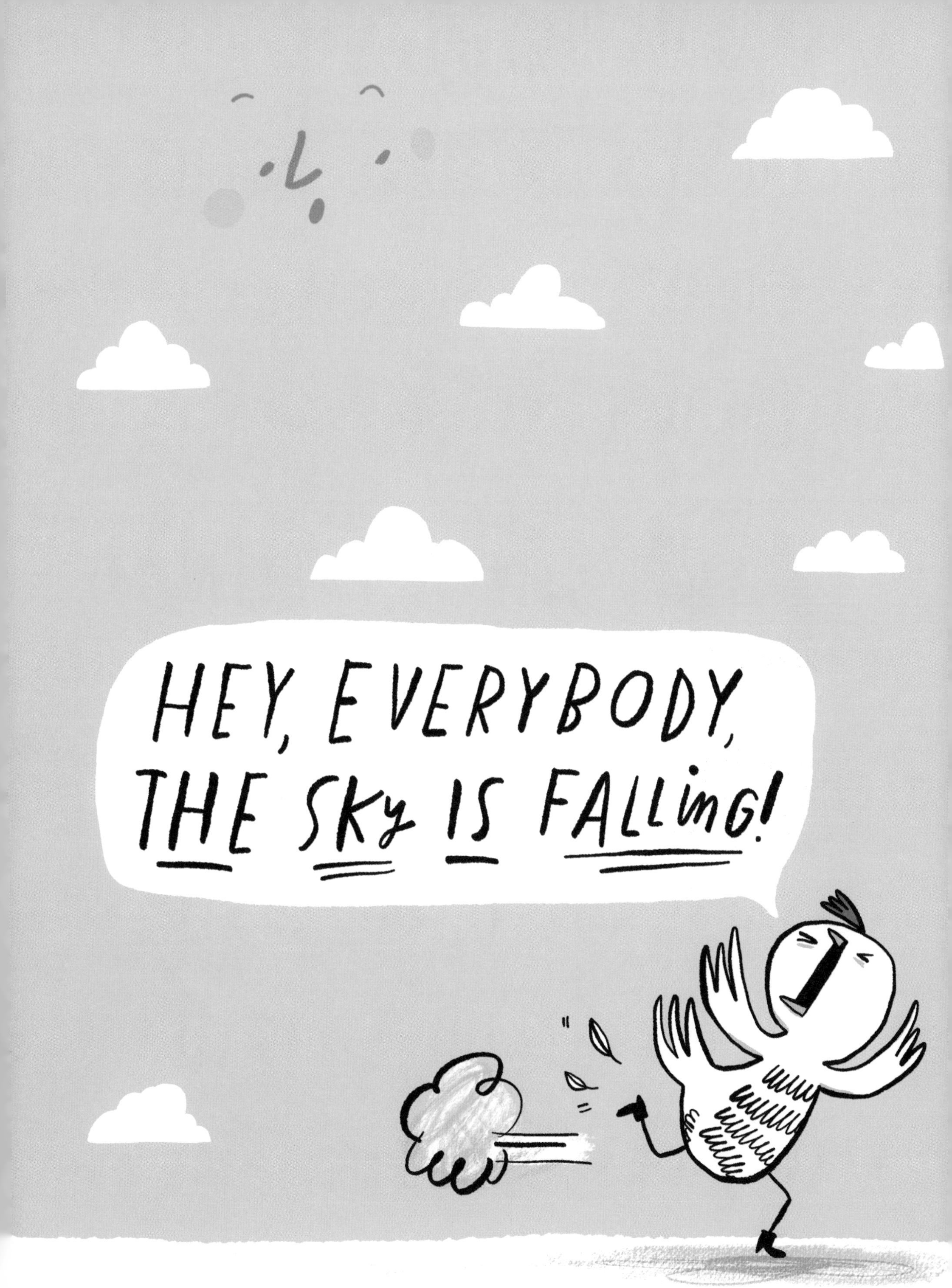
HEY, EVERYBODY, THE SKY IS FALLING!

THE SKY IS FALLING!

RUN! RUN!! RUN!!!

THE SKY IS

RUUUUUUUUU

FALLING!

UUUUUUUUN!!!

CHICKEN LITTLE BROUGHT in the FACT-
CHECKING SNIPES, WHO WERE WIDELY
RESPECTED, BUT the HORDE of
HENS WOULD'NT STOP TO LISTEN.

CHICKEN LITTLE TRIED to
CORRAL THEM INTO THE COOP SO
SHE COULD EXPLAIN.

BUT THE CHICKENS REFUSED to
BE CAGED.

THINGS REALLY GOT OUT
OF HAND WHEN CHICKEN LITTLE
HEARD THE HENS CHANTING
"CUT THE FENCE!
CUT THE FENCE!"

AND SHE WAS.

SEE?! TOLD YOU I WASN'T AFRAID OF ANYTHING!

FOR MAX + ALISTAIR + RUSS

• Library of Congress Cataloging-in-Publication Data available •
ISBN 978-1-338-35901-5 • 10 9 8 7 6 5 4 3 2 1   20 21 22 23 24 • Printed in China   62 • First edition, May 2020
Sam Wedelich's illustrations were created digitally. • The type was hand lettered by Sam Wedelich. • The set type is Amatic Regular. The book was printed on 120gsm woodfree and bound at Leo Paper. • Production was overseen by Catherine Weening. • Manufacturing was supervised by Shannon Rice. • The book was art directed and designed by Marijka Kostiw and edited by Tracy Mack.

YOU MUST
BE THIS TALL
TO RIDE